MAY 13 '98

Dragon's Easter Egg Hunt

SCHOLASTIC READER LEVEL 1 50-250 WORDS

Adapted by Mae Marks
Based on an original TV episode written by Steve Westren

SCHOLASTIC INC.
New York   Toronto   London   Auckland
Sydney   Mexico City   New Delhi   Hong Kong

ISBN 978-0-545-20060-8

12 11 10 9 8 7 6 5 4 3 2 1   12 13 14 15 16 17/0

Printed in the U.S.A. 40
First printing, March 2012

It was a spring day.
Dragon was outside.

Alligator came to visit.
He brought bunny ears
and candy eggs.

"Let's have an Easter egg hunt,"
said Alligator.

"I will be the Easter Bunny," said Dragon.
"I will hide the eggs."

"Remember not to eat the eggs,"
Alligator said.

Dragon loved candy.
But he promised
not to eat the eggs.

**Next Dragon put on
a bunny tail.**

**Then Dragon put on
a bunny nose.**

"Now I look like the Easter Bunny," Dragon said.

Dragon was ready
to hide the eggs.

Dragon thought about eating the eggs.

They looked yummy.

Dragon had an idea!
He dressed up the eggs.

Now the eggs would
look like cat toys!
Dragon would not
want to eat toys.

Then Dragon hid the eggs.

Mailmouse, Alligator, Beaver, and Ostrich looked for the eggs.

Mailmouse looked in the mailbox.
She could not find any eggs.

Alligator looked near the trash can.
He could not find any eggs.

Ostrich and Beaver could not find any eggs.

"Where are all the eggs?"
asked Dragon.

Later Dragon went inside
to feed Cat.

Look! Dragon found the eggs!

Cat thought the eggs were cat toys.

Dragon hid the Easter eggs again.

The friends found all the eggs.

"Happy Easter!" said Dragon.